Puddle Pug

by
KIM NORMAN

illustrated by
KEIKA YAMAGUCHI

STERLING CHILDREN'S BOOKS
New York

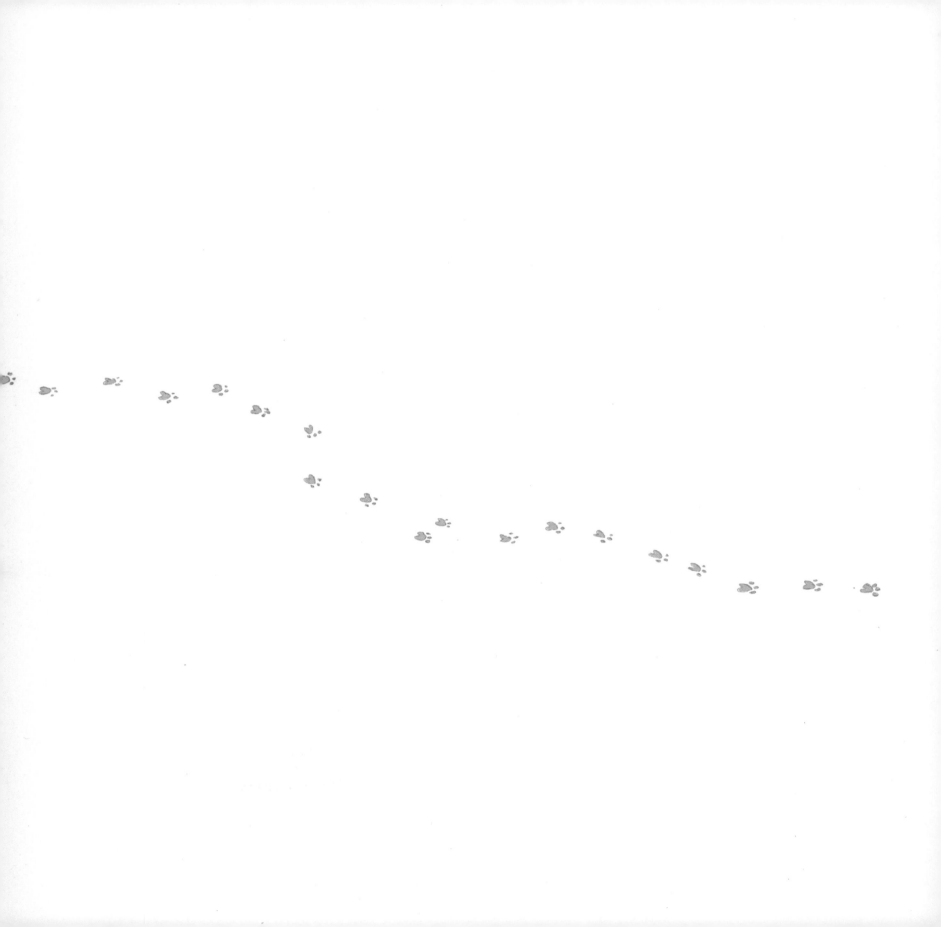

For Moira, who always helps me think outside the puddle, in memory of Sniffles. —K.N.

For my parents, Sumiko and Koshiro, who always have been supportive
of my passion to pursue my dreams. —K.Y.

STERLING CHILDREN'S BOOKS
New York

An Imprint of Sterling Publishing
387 Park Avenue South
New York, NY 10016

STERLING CHILDREN'S BOOKS and the distinctive Sterling Children's Books logo are trademarks of Sterling Publishing Co., Inc.

Text © 2014 by Kim Norman
Illustrations © 2014 by Keika Yamaguchi
Art direction and design by Merideth Harte

The illustrations were drawn with pencil and painted digitally.

ISBN 978-1-4549-0436-6
Library of Congress Cataloging-in-Publication Data

Norman, Kim.
 Puddle pug / by Kim Norman ; illustrated by Keika Yamaguchi.
   pages cm
 Summary: Percy the pug searches far and wide for the perfect puddle but when he finds it, Mama pig is unhappy about him joining her family until a storm provides Percy the opportunity to prove himself to her.
  ISBN 978-1-4549-0436-6
 [1. Pug--Fiction. 2. Dogs--Fiction. 3. Pigs--Fiction.] I. Yamaguchi, Keika, illustrator. II. Title.
 PZ7.N7846Pud 2014
 [E]--dc23

      2013018894

Distributed in Canada by Sterling Publishing
c/o Canadian Manda Group, 165 Dufferin Street
Toronto, Ontario, Canada M6K 3H6
Distributed in the United Kingdom by GMC Distribution Services
Castle Place, 166 High Street, Lewes, East Sussex, England BN7 1XU
Distributed in Australia by Capricorn Link (Australia) Pty. Ltd.
P.O. Box 704, Windsor, NSW 2756, Australia

For information about custom editions, special sales, and premium and corporate purchases,
please contact Sterling Special Sales at 800-805-5489 or specialsales@sterlingpublishing.com.

Manufactured in China
Lot #:
2 4 6 8 10 9 7 5 3 1
01/14

www.sterlingpublishing.com/kids

Percy was a puddle pug.
He loved puddles of every sort:

Swamp puddles,

stomp puddles,

ready-for-a-romp puddles.

Foggy puddles,

froggy puddles,

deeper-than-a-doggy puddles.

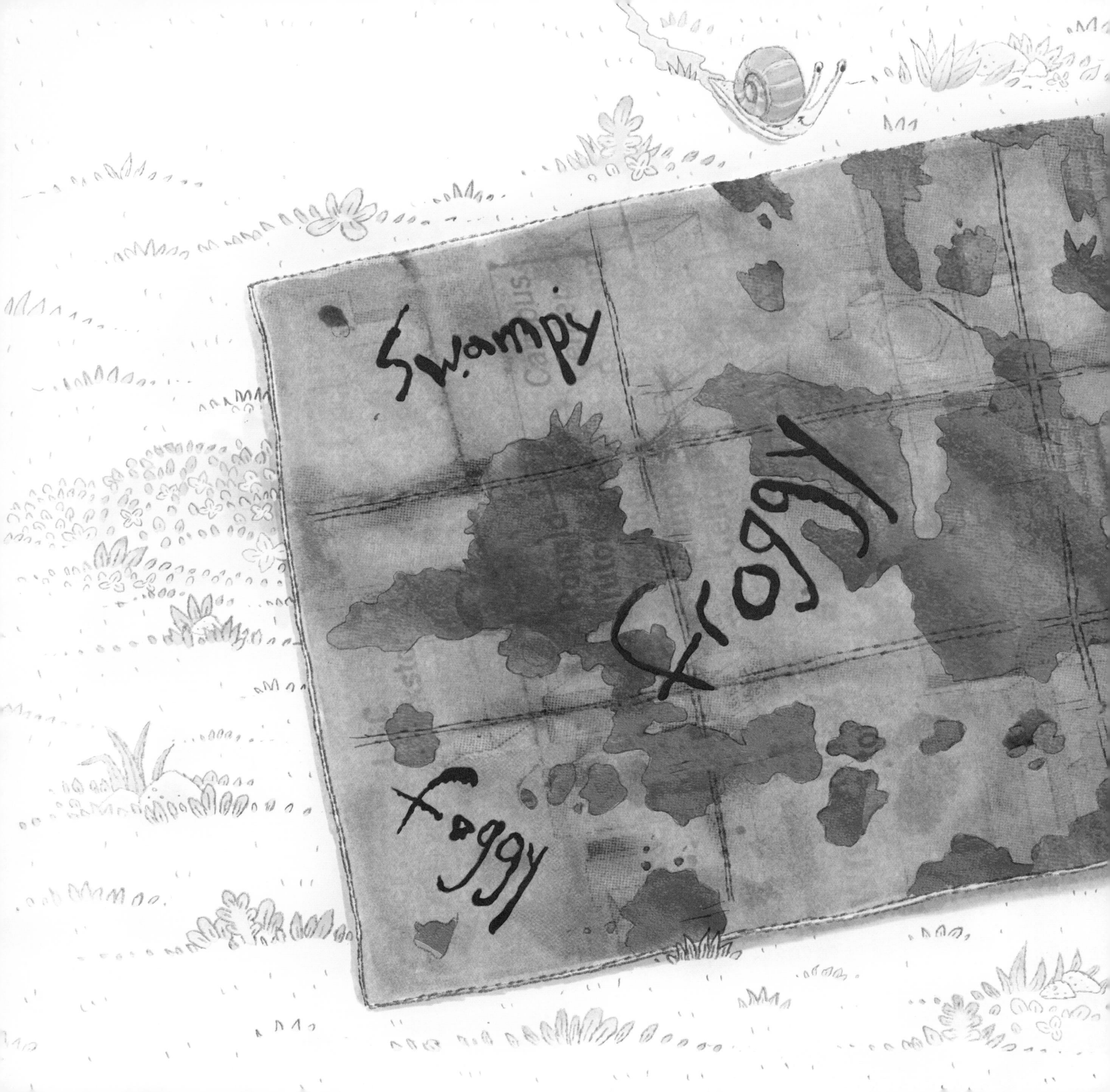
Swampy
Froggy
Foggy

Percy loved puddles so much he put them on
a map so he could remember where to find them.

All of Percy's puddles were pleasing, but he had yet to find the perfect puddle. Some were NEARLY perfect,

like this one . . .

and this one . . .

and this one . . .

. . . but something was always missing.

One day Percy heard splashing on
the other side of the fence.
He peered through, and there it was:

The PERFECT puddle.
It was big. It was brown.
And it was oh so *friendly*.
Percy couldn't resist.

He squeezed under the fence and . . .

SPLASH!

Oooh . . .
Cool, brown water.
Ahhh . . .
Squishy, swishy mud.
It was puddle paradise.

Percy loved his new puddle.

But his puddle did not love him back.

Percy couldn't get that perfect puddle out of his head.
On his daily walk, he couldn't enjoy the puddles he DID find.

Too buggy.

Too sluggy.

Too tiny.

Too spiny.

Too smelly.

Too yelly.

Too endless.

Too . . . friendless.

PIGS
ONLY

Only one puddle was juuuust right . . .
and it was behind that fence.

Maybe I could blend in, Percy thought.

Mama's eye twitched.

Percy tried sharing a tasty treat.

Mama's nose twitched.

He even tried an underwater route.

Mama's tail twitched . . .

. . . and she pitched Percy out of the puddle!

The next day, Percy felt a drop of water on his head.
Oh, good! Rain means more puddles, he thought.
But then the wind began to whistle through the
branches of the old tree. The whistle grew to a howl.
Overhead, Percy heard a different sound. *CRACK!!*

Pigs and pug scattered as the tree
crashed into the wallow.

By sundown, Mama Pig had found all but one of her piglets. Where was teeny, tiny Petunia?

Petunia was too tiny to be gone so long. *Where would a too-tiny pig go?* Percy wondered.

He stared at his puddle map.
Then he remembered the *perfect* place for a
too-tiny pig . . . in the too-tiny puddle!

When Percy pranced through the fence with Petunia on his back, Mama's whole *body* twitched—with piggly jiggly JOY!

Percy is a puddle pug.
He loves puddles of every sort:

Blue puddles,

dew puddles,

thick as turtle
stew puddles.

Wide puddles,

tide puddles,

even partly dried puddles.

But there's one perfect puddle
he loves the most.

And Percy's puddle loves him right back.